little bee books

An imprint of Bonnier Publishing USA
251 Park Avenue South, New York, NY 10010
Copyright © 2018 by Little Bee Books
All rights reserved, including the right of reproduction in whole or
in part in any form.
Little Bee Books is a trademark of Bonnier Publishing USA, and
associated colophon is a trademark of Bonnier Publishing USA.

Library of Congress Cataloging-in-Publication Data
Names: Reed, Melody, author. | Pépin, Émilie, illustrator.
Title: Battle of the bands / by Melody Reed; illustrated by Émilie Pépin.
Description: First edition. | New York, NY: Little Bee Books, [2018].
Series: The major eights; #1 | Summary: Keyboardist Jasmine, age eight, tries
to convince her bandmates, Maggie, Becca, and Scarlet, to prove themselves
in a Battle of the Bands competition, despite their poor equipment.
Identifiers: LCCN 2017004961 | Subjects: | CYAC: Bands (Music)—Fiction. |
Friendship—Fiction. | Contests—Fiction. | Chinese Americans—Fiction. |
BISAC: JUVENILE FICTION / Readers / Chapter Books. | JUVENILE FICTION /
Performing Arts / Music. | JUVENILE FICTION / Girls & Women. |
Classification: LCC PZ7.1.R428 Bat 2018
DDC [Fic]—dc23 | LC record available at https://lccn.loc.gov/2017004961

Printed in the United States of America LAK 1217
ISBN 978-1-4998-0565-9 (hc)
First Edition 10 9 8 7 6 5 4 3 2 1
ISBN 978-1-4998-0564-2 (pb)
First Edition 10 9 8 7 6 5 4 3 2 1
littlebeebooks.com
bonnierpublishingusa.com

THE MAJOR EIGHTS

BATTLE OF THE BANDS

by Melody Reed
illustrated by Émilie Pépin

little bee books

CONTENTS

1. THE PERFECT IDEA 1

2. A REAL BAND 11

3. OOPS 17

4. LET'S DO IT! 23

5. THE REAL SONG 31

6. A BIG IDEA 45

7. FOX POX 51

8. BATTLE OF THE BANDS 69

9. AND THE WINNER IS 85

THE PERFECT IDEA

"Hit it, Jasmine!" said Scarlet. She tossed her braids. Beads clicked against one another.

"You got it," I said. I put my fingers on the keyboard. It has five keys that do not work. No sound comes out of them. We have a piano upstairs that doesn't have any broken keys, but I wanted to be in the basement, where I could jam with my friends.

1

"Wait!" Becca called. "Can you play an E first?"

"Sure," I said. I found the note. The keyboard hummed a low E.

Becca twisted a peg on her guitar. She plucked a string, over and over. It finally sounded like the keyboard. Then she tuned the other strings.

Maggie sat behind my dad's old drum set. She twirled one of her drumsticks. It spun out of her hand and hit the floor. "Oops," she said.

2

"I'll get it!" Scarlet yelled. She handed the stick to Maggie. Then Scarlet began warming up her voice. "Do, mi, so, do, mi, so, do," she sang. We don't have a mic in my basement, but Scarlet's aunt has one. She is a singer. (Wow!) At my house, Scarlet sings into my hairbrush. She likes to practice with something in her hand.

"Ready," said Becca.

"Me, too," called Maggie.

"I was *born* ready," Scarlet said confidently.

"Here we go!" I said.

3

I played the notes in a chord, one at a time. Then I moved on to another chord. I tried to keep the beat even.

Maggie took up the beat on her kick drum.

Becca watched my hands. She strummed her guitar to fit the rhythm.

At first, Scarlet listened. Then she sang: "Once I was inside a *box*. There I met a crazy *fox*. He told me I had chicken *pox*—"

Maggie bent over and giggled. Her foot slid off the pedal for the kick drum.

Scarlet turned to face her, singing, "Maggie, we need that *beat*, or else you have to smell my *feet*!"

Maggie fell on the floor laughing. She rolled on the carpet. Her red curls spilled around her head.

I laughed so hard my stomach hurt.

"Five minutes, Jasmine!" my mom called down.

"Okay," I called back. I turned to my friends. "Sorry, guys. I have to go eat dinner."

"No problem," Maggie said. She stood up. "I need to study for our science test."

"You already did," I said.

Maggie tied her sneakers. "I just need to make *sure* I get an A."

Becca unzipped a soft, guitar-shaped bag. She put her guitar inside.

"Hey," she said. "My brother gave me his old gig bag." She held it up. "Cool, right? I look like a real musician."

"You *are* a real musician," Scarlet said. She gave me back my hairbrush.

"We *all* are."

We went up the stairs together. "Do you want to come over tomorrow?" I asked my friends. "After I get home from Chinese school?"

"Of course," said Becca.

"Perfect," said Maggie.

"Always," said Scarlet.

A REAL BAND

Mom passed the bowl of beef chow fun to my brother, Nick. Nick still wore his football uniform. He smelled like dirty socks. I wrinkled my nose.

"How was school today, Jasmine?" Mom asked.

"Fine," I said. I put noodles on my plate. "But band practice was *way* more fun."

"Practice?" Nick said. "No, *I* have practices. *You* just have fun with your friends."

"Nick, be nice," Dad warned.

My cheeks heated. "Our band is more than that," I said. "We're good."

"If you're so good," Nick said, "why don't you enter the Battle of the Bands?"

I glared at him. "What is that?"

"Nick," Dad warned again. He turned to me. "Center City is having a competition this year. They call it the Battle of the Bands. But it's not just for bands. Any musician can enter. All the entrants will perform at the Fall Festival. The winner gets a thousand dollars."

I sat up straight. "A *thousand* dollars?"

Nick took a bite of his noodles. "I was just kidding, Jasmine," he said with his mouth full. "The Battle of the Bands is for older people. Not eight-year-olds. I know some guys at my high school that are entering."

I narrowed my eyes at him. "We could do it."

"*Sure* you could," Nick said. "But has your band even played a real song? Like, a song by a real band? A  song you might hear on the radio?"

I thought about it. We *were* a band, after all. Bands perform. What if we *did* enter the Battle of the Bands?

14

Sure, we would need to learn a real song. But if we won, I could get a new keyboard. Or a mic. Or a sound system. And we could show everyone that we were a real band.

This was the perfect idea. Now all I had to do was talk to Becca, Maggie, and Scarlet. I had to make *them* think it was the perfect idea, too.

OOPS

The next morning, I sat at my desk. I chewed on a fingernail. What would Becca, Maggie, and Scarlet think? We *had* to do the Battle of the Bands. I peeled off a piece of pink nail polish. But maybe Nick was right. Maybe eight-year-olds couldn't do it.

My band friends and I all go to the same school. But none of us are in the same third-grade class. My best friend in my class is Leslie Miller.

She gets good grades, and she is really good at piano. She almost always beats me at piano competitions. Sometimes I feel jealous that she's so good at piano. But she's my friend, so I try not to let it bother me.

"Good morning, class," said Ms. Kwan.

Leslie sat up straight.

"I want to begin with a special announcement," Ms. Kwan said. "This year at Center City's Fall Festival, there will be a Battle of the Bands."

My ears perked up.

"I will be helping with it." She beamed at us. "And Leslie has just told me she will be entering the competition on piano."

My mouth dropped open. Leslie grinned.

I shot up out of my chair. "We are, too!" I shouted. "And we are going to win!"

The class got quiet. Ms. Kwan blinked. My face got hot.

"I . . . oh. Is that so, Jasmine?" Ms. Kwan said.

Everyone stared at me. I sat back down. "Um, yes," I said quietly.

Ms. Kwan smiled. "That's wonderful, Jasmine. And who is 'we'?"

I swallowed. "Um, my band," I said.

"Fantastic," Ms. Kwan said. She pulled out her laptop. "I will add you to the list."

My stomach tightened. Now I *really* had to convince Becca, Maggie, and Scarlet.

4

LET'S DO IT!

"The Battle of the Bands?" said Scarlet.

"I don't know. . . . " said Maggie.

"Isn't that for grown-ups?" asked Becca.

I took a deep breath. A ball bounced past us. Kids shouted from the monkey bars. "We said last night we were a real band," I said. "And if we win, we can buy stuff to make us better. Like a mic. Or a keyboard. Or speakers."

"I have those things," Scarlet said.

"Me, too," said Becca. "But my brother is always using them."

Scarlet nodded. "Yeah," she said. "My aunt is always using hers."

"See?" I said. "If we had our own, we could use those things whenever we wanted!"

Maggie frowned. "I still don't think . . ."

"Hi, Jasmine." It was Leslie. Her friends stood behind her. They all wore pigtails with ribbons.

"Hi, Leslie," I said.

"So, you're doing the Battle of the Bands, too? That's great!" said Leslie.

"No, we are only talking about it," Becca said.

"Oh," said Leslie. "But Jasmine told Ms. Kwan you were doing it."

I slapped my forehead.

"Jasmine!!!" said Becca.

Scarlet put her hands on her hips.

Maggie's eyes got big.

Leslie looked embarrassed. "Well, I hope to see you there." She and her friends walked away. Their pigtails all bounced together.

Oops.

"I'm sorry," I told my friends.

Scarlet folded her arms. Becca and Maggie frowned.

"The truth is," I said, "we are a good band. And this would be fun. We can prove to everyone that being *eight* is *great*, and we can do anything anyone else can!"

My friends looked at each other.

Scarlet grinned. "Why not?"

Maggie took a deep breath. "If you say so."

Becca shrugged. "Okay, I'm in."

I smiled. My friends were convinced. We were doing the Battle of the Bands!

5

THE REAL SONG

On Friday night, we practiced in Scarlet's aunt's basement, which is our favorite place to play. Her aunt has a real recording studio there. She uses it a lot, but sometimes she lets us practice there.

"First things first," I said. "Every band has a name. We need one."

"No kidding," said Scarlet. "But what?"

"I know! We are all eight," said Maggie. "We could be the Eight-Year-Olds."

Scarlet scrunched up her nose. "I don't know. . . ."

"How about the Pink and Purple Ping-Pong Paddles?" I asked. "Pink is the best color in the world."

"And purple is, too," Scarlet agreed.

"I don't like pink," said Becca. "Black is the best color ever."

"I like blue best," said Maggie.

I sighed. "Well, we can't be the Black and Blue Ping-Pong Paddles. That sounds like we have bruises."

"How about the Centers? After Center City?" asked Becca.

"Cute," I said.

"But it sounds like a sports team," said Scarlet.

"So?" Becca put her hands on her hips.

"So, we are not a sports team," said Scarlet. "What about the Basement Bandits?"

Maggie nodded in agreement. "We do practice in basements."

"Except when we play in my garage," said Becca. "I like Maggie's idea. We should do something with 'eight.'"

"But what?" said Scarlet.

We thought. But none of us came up with anything.

"Maybe we should practice first," I said. "We can pick a name later."

My friends nodded. I passed out sheet music.

"What is this?" asked Scarlet.

I smiled. "My mom took me to the music store today. I got us a song to play for the Battle of the Bands!"

"A real song?" asked Maggie. She stared at the sheet. She wrinkled her nose at it.

"Yes," I said. "To compete, we need to do a real song. I always learn real songs for my piano competitions. So does Leslie. I know she'll play a real song at the Battle of the Bands."

Becca's voice rose. "But I can't read music!"

"Well," I said. I hadn't thought about that.

"I guess just watch my hands again."

"But this is *piano* sheet music." Maggie waved the sheet at me. "There's nothing for drums on it."

I swallowed. I hadn't thought about that, either. "Well," I said. "I guess just find the beat like you always do."

I sat down behind Scarlet's aunt's keyboard. It looked so nice and new. I couldn't wait to play. "Okay, let's try it," I said.

I looked at the music. There were a lot of notes. I decided to play only the right hand to start with.

Scarlet began singing.

"Your love is like a song . . . to the beat of my heart. . . ."

It was awful. It didn't sound like the song on the radio at all.

Scarlet stopped. I was the only one playing. "We just need practice," I told my friends.

"This is a *love* song." Scarlet made a face. "Gross!"

"And you aren't playing with your left hand," said Becca. "That's where I watch for chords."

"Just keep playing," said Maggie. "We'll get it."

Scarlet shrugged. "Also, I only know the chorus."

I frowned. "Maybe we should skip ahead, then."

I played the chorus. Scarlet belted out the high notes. Maggie picked up the beat on the kick drum. Becca looked over my shoulder. It finally started to sound like the song! Maybe this would work after all.

But Becca still did not play. Finally, she took off the guitar strap. She put her guitar away in its gig bag.

We all stopped.

"What's wrong?" Scarlet asked her.

Becca's face turned red. "I can't play this!" she shouted.

I blinked. Maggie dropped her sticks. Scarlet raised her eyebrows.

"I told you," Becca said. "I only read chords Major chords, minor chords. But I do not read music. This is too hard!" She zipped the bag shut.

"Wait!" I cried. "Becca, I know it's hard. But we can figure it out. We have to. We need to play a real song!"

"Then I guess I am not competing," Becca said. She threw the gig bag over her shoulder. She stormed up the stairs. The door slammed shut behind her.

"Now what do we do?" Maggie asked.

"We can't compete without a guitar," I said.

"We are not a *band* without a guitar," Scarlet said.

"We are not a band without *Becca*," Maggie said.

My heart sank. Competing in the Battle of the Bands was going to be harder than I thought.

6

A BIG IDEA

Scarlet, Maggie, and I practiced without Becca. We practiced for several days. But the real song still did not sound right. The piano part was too hard for me. Scarlet didn't know the tune, so she made up her own. Maggie only played her kick drum, because she was afraid of playing the song wrong.

And we all missed Becca.

Later that week, Mom was driving me home from school.

"I haven't seen Becca lately," said Mom.

I leaned my cheek against the door. "Me neither."

"Is she still in the band?" Mom asked.

"No," I said. "She left because she didn't like the song I picked for us to play."

"Hmm," said Mom. "That sounds tricky."

"It is." I sighed. "We sound awful without her. The Battle of the Bands is in one week."

"Maybe you don't need to win," said Mom. "Maybe you should just go up there and have fun."

"But if we win, we can buy equipment. If we win, we will show everyone that we are a real band."

"I think you already *are* a real band, Jasmine. And I think you and your friends are at your best when you are having fun. Together."

I thought about what Mom said. Nobody had fun with the song I picked. Especially Becca.

And then I had an idea.

"Mom! Do you have any paper?"

Fox Pox

"So, what's so important, Jasmine?"
Scarlet folded her arms. It was the
next night. At recess that day, I had
told my band friends to come over for
a super-important meeting. I had the
broken keyboard and hairbrush mic
ready. Maggie sat behind the drums.
Even Becca came. But she sat on the
basement stairs.

I took a deep breath. "I want us to have fun again," I said.

Scarlet and Maggie looked at each other.

"Ever since we started playing the song I picked, we've been fighting. Becca got mad and left. We aren't having fun anymore."

Scarlet nodded. "I don't like the song," she said. "You picked it without asking us."

Maggie whispered, "It is a hard song, too."

"And there are no chords for Becca," Scarlet said.

"I know," I said. "I thought we had to do a hard song to win. But it doesn't matter if we win. I just want my friends back."

Becca came down the steps. "I'm sorry I left," she said. She hugged me. Then Scarlet hugged both of us. Then Maggie hugged all of us. We were a giant dumpling, all squished together. I laughed. Scarlet laughed.

Maggie and Becca laughed. We bobbled against each other and Maggie tripped. We all went down with her. We were a pile of giggles on the carpet.

I sat up. It was good to have all my friends back. Now I had to tell them my new idea.

"I have something else to say," I said.

My friends listened.

I pulled out sheets of paper. Maggie and Scarlet frowned. Becca glanced up the stairs.

"It's not what you think," I said. I passed out the pages. "I wrote down the song we made up last week.

It's not for the competition or anything. It's just for fun. I created a chorus and verses. And I put in guitar chords." I smiled at Becca.

She looked at the paper. "I can play this!"

"Hey," said Scarlet. "These are the words I was singing!"

"We should do this!" said Maggie.

Becca took her guitar out. I played notes for her to tune to. Maggie rolled on her snare drum to warm up. Scarlet sang her scales.

"We sound crazy!" I said.

Scarlet laughed. "Hit it, Jasmine!"

I strung out the notes in the first chord, E major. I played them one at a time, counting the beats.

Maggie joined me. She pressed the kick drum pedal in time with the beat.

Becca strummed along with us. Her face glowed.

Scarlet began to sing. "Once I was inside a box. There I met a crazy fox. He told me I had chicken pox. But I said . . ."

We built up to the chorus. Becca, Maggie, and I paused. Then we played loud. Scarlet sang: "People get chicken pox, chickens get fox pox, foxes get people pox. That's a lot of crazy talk. . . ."

Maggie giggled. But she kept the beat.

For the first time, we played a whole song together. It was not a *real* song, but it was *our* song. And that was even better.

"Hey," Scarlet said. "What if we play that song at the Battle of the Bands?"

I frowned. "But I just wrote it down for fun."

"We definitely should! It's a great song," Becca said. "And we wrote it!"

Maggie nodded. "Let's do it!"

I didn't know what to say. I thought we were just being silly together. Singing this in front of a crowd was *not* my plan. Then again, my friends were happy. "Well . . ."

"Come on, Jasmine," they begged. "Please?"

I shrugged. "Oh, okay."

Maggie and Becca high-fived. Scarlet said, "That song is majorly funny."

"That's it!" shouted Maggie. "We can be the Major Eights! You know, 'major' like 'major chords' and also like . . . 'important.'" She put her hands on her hips like a superhero.

"That and we're *majorly* crazy," Scarlet laughed.

"That's perfect!" Becca said.

"Yeah," I said. But inside, I was worried. If we played this song for the competition, people would laugh at us. My brother would make fun of me. Leslie would beat me again. And people would not believe we were a real band.

This was *not* looking good.

BATTLE OF THE BANDS

I took a deep breath. The air smelled like corn dogs. From behind the stage, we could hear Leslie Miller playing her piano solo. Ms. Kwan stood ready with her laptop. Mom and Dad and Nick were out there watching. I huddled closer to Scarlet, Becca, and Maggie.

"We're still doing 'Fox Pox,' right?" Scarlet whispered.

"Definitely," Becca said.

I still had time to change their minds. "Maybe we should do the other one."

"What?!" they all whispered.

"It's just . . . listen to Leslie! She sounds like . . . a grown-up."

Leslie finished her solo. The crowd cheered.

Ms. Kwan nodded to the next group. They were a lot older than us. They wore black leather. The girl with the keyboard even had pink hair. They carried a sign that said, Silver Sporks.

Maggie said, "Maybe Jasmine is right."

"But . . . I can't play the other song!" Becca said. "I thought we were doing 'Fox Pox.'"

"Me, too," said Scarlet.

Then the Silver Sporks began. "Your love is like a song . . . to the beat of my heart. . . ."

I stomped my foot. "That's *our* song!"

"Oh, no!" said Maggie.

I listened. "They play it better than we do," I said.

"Jasmine," said Becca, "we *have* to play 'Fox Pox now.'"

"But it's just a crazy song we made up on the spot," I said. "It was just for fun!"

"That's right," said Scarlet. "It *is* fun. Which is why I want to do it."

"Me, too," said Becca.

"Me three," said Maggie.

I sighed. "But we might lose," I said.

"That doesn't matter," said Scarlet.

"They'll laugh at us," I said.

"It's a funny song!" Becca replied.

"They will think we're not a real band," I said.

"So what?" said Maggie. "Jasmine, there's no time left!"

The Silver Sporks finished their song. Ms. Kwan called us over. Becca, Maggie, and Scarlet bounced onto the stage.

I hung my head. The Silver Sporks high-fived us on their way down the stairs. The keyboard girl with pink hair looked at me. She smiled and said, "Hey, break a finger."

"What?" I asked, surprised.

"She was being silly," Becca whispered. "She meant 'good luck.'"

We took our places on the stage. I stared out at the crowd. My parents and Nick were in the front. My heart sped up.

But if the Silver Sporks could be silly and still be good, maybe we could, too. I looked up. Scarlet stood proudly, mic in hand. Becca had her guitar strapped on. Maggie smiled from the drum set. I smiled back.

Ms. Kwan announced, "And now, the Major Eights!" The crowd clapped politely.

I began the chords. I played each note, one at a time. Becca and Maggie joined in.

Then Scarlet began to sing.

At first, the crowd was quiet. But slowly, the laughter started. It spread through the crowd. My face got hot.

I felt like running off the stage. But my friends kept playing. When we got to the chorus and Scarlet sang about fox pox, the laughter erupted. Everyone laughed. I looked down as I played. I could not wait for the song to be over.

And then, it was. The crowd did not laugh anymore. They cheered! My mouth fell open. They had not been laughing *at* us. They were laughing *with* us. They thought our song was funny!

My parents cheered in the front. Even Nick cheered. He shouted, "Go, Jasmine! The Major Eights rock!!!"

I beamed with pride.

Ms. Kwan smiled wide at us. "Great job, girls!"

The four of us stood together, arm in arm. We took a bow. The crowd cheered even louder. Someone whistled.

"I can't believe this is happening!"
Maggie said.

"They really like us," Becca said.

"Of course they do!" Scarlet agreed.

"This is the best day ever!" I yelled.

AND THE WINNER IS...

Becca, Scarlet, Maggie, and I waited.
We had waited all day for this.

Leslie came over. "Jasmine, your
band was great!" she said.

"Not as good as your piano solo," I
told her. "But thanks!"

Finally, Ms. Kwan was onstage. She held a paper in her hand. "I have the results from the judges," she announced. "For Center City's Battle of the Bands, the grand prize winner of the thousand dollars is . . . "

Maggie crossed her fingers. Scarlet held her breath. Becca and I squeezed each other's hands.

". . . the Silver Sporks!"

Our shoulders sagged. But the
Silver Sporks seemed like a nice group.
I clapped for them. I was glad they
won.

"It is really okay that we didn't win," Becca said.

"Maybe we can enter another one of these sometime," Maggie said.

"I would like that," I agreed.

"Me, too," Scarlet said.

But Ms. Kwan was not finished. After the Silver Sporks got their check, she stepped up to the mic again. "We also have an honorable mention to award," she said.

"What's that?" I whispered.

"Somebody who was pretty good, but didn't win," Maggie whispered back.

"The judges think this group has a lot of potential," said Ms. Kwan. "And I think we can all agree that they do. The honorable mention goes to . . ."

". . . the Major Eights!"

Scarlet screamed. Becca jumped in the air. Maggie's jaw dropped.

"That's us!" I shouted.

"Come on," Scarlet said. We ran up onstage, panting for breath.

"Girls, we were so impressed with your song," Ms. Kwan said into the mic. "Tell us, who wrote it?"

Becca looked at Scarlet. Maggie giggled. Scarlet grinned and looked at me.

I spoke into the mic. "We, uh . . . all did," I said. "The four of us."

"Amazing!" said Ms. Kwan. "So tell us, will we be seeing more of the Major Eights?"

We looked at each other and smiled. Together we answered, "Absolutely!"

Read on for a sneak peek from the second book in **THE MAJOR EiGHTS** series, *Scarlet's Big Break*.

OH, SAY, CAN YOU SING?

It all began the week after the Battle of the Bands.

I was sitting in the bleachers on Saturday morning, watching my little brother Tyson's baseball game. Wind shook the leaves on the trees. I wished the sun would come out.

Then Coach Suarez walked over. "Scarlet, right?" she asked.

I jumped up. "What?"

"From the Major Eights? At the Battle of the Bands?" asked Coach Suarez.

Jasmine, Becca, Maggie, and I hadn't won the competition. But the crowd had loved us. We got an honorable mention. And we'd had a blast.

I blinked. "That's me."

"Do you know the national anthem?" she asked.

"Of course," I answered Coach Suarez. I looked over at Aunt Billie. She stood near my parents, watching Tyson. Aunt Billie lives just two blocks away from us. She's not only my aunt; she's also my singing coach. She grinned at me from the fence.

"Would you sing it this morning? To start the game?" Coach Suarez asked. "I just got a call. The woman who was going to sing for us today is sick."

My eyes bugged out. *"Really?"* Now I really jumped up. "You want me to sing? Here?"

"You girls did a great job last week," Coach Suarez said. "The whole town's talking about it."

When it comes to singing, nobody needs to ask me twice. "I'll do it!" I said. "Do you have a mic?"

"We have a PA system over here."

"Then let's do this!" I skipped down the bleachers.

And just like that, I had my first solo gig.

Coach Suarez left to prep the PA system.

Aunt Billie came over. "See?" she whispered. "The one song every singer needs to know. You never know when you'll need it." Aunt Billie was named after a famous singer. She is a singer, too. A really good one.

Coach Suarez passed me the mic. The crowd got quiet. Even the five-year-old ballplayers held still. We all turned to face the flag.

I started to sing. "Oh, say, can you see. . . ."

But then the mic cut out!

My eyes got big. I kept singing anyway. I acted like it was fine.

". . . By the dawn's early light. . . ."

The mic *still* didn't work. Wind blew across it, and it picked that up just fine.

But I kept on singing.

I paused after "ramparts." I'd had enough of this mic.

I set the mic down. I turned and faced the crowd and belted out the rest.

At ". . . la-and of the *FREE*," I was in the zone. People clapped and hooted. I finished the song: ". . . and the hooooome . . . of the . . . braaaaaaave!"

The crowd cheered.

Tyson pointed at me. He yelled, "That's my sister!"

Still clapping, Coach Suarez made a face. "Sorry about the microphone. You handled it great, though!"

"What a pro!" said a parent.

Coach Suarez dug in her purse. She handed me an orange piece of paper. "Have you heard about this?" she asked. "My kids go to your school. I saw this yesterday."

I read the flyer aloud: "Enter the talent show! Bring your tutus. Bring your routines. Bring your voice!" My heart sped up. "A week from Friday, 7pm. In the gym. Come be a superstar!"

Wow.

A picture popped into my head. I was in the spotlight. I was singing at that talent show. And everybody in the whole school cheered! I grinned.

"Thanks," I said to Coach Suarez.

She squeezed my shoulder and left.

I hugged the flyer. Maybe I could sing alone, like my aunt. Maybe I could even win. Maybe . . .

Kids grabbed their gloves. They lined up. Coach Suarez ushered them out onto the field.

Maybe . . . maybe *I* could be a superstar!